Underneath the Surface

Tanya Gandolfo

Editing by Lorna Lee Earl
Book Cover Design by Peter O' Conner

ISBN 978-0-6482956-0-0 (Paperback)
ISBN 978-0-6482956-1-7 (Epub)
ISBN 978-0-6482956-2-4 (Mobi)

Acknowledgements

Thank you to all my friends and family, to everyone who has helped me every step of the way to make this a reality. You all mean so much to me and I couldn't have done this without you all by my side.

Prologue

I clutched onto my mum's faded jeans as she glanced around the courtyard. Many families were saying goodbye to their children. I was one of them. I glanced around the courtyard until I made accidental eye contact with a young boy who was screaming at his parents. They bent down to his eye level, trying to calm him down but their attempts were useless. His cries grew louder until they were the only thing you could hear. He grabbed at his parents, his small fingers grasping at them when one of the male teachers grabbed him. He struggled within the man's arms, kicking and screaming as he was hauled away. My cheeks warmed with tears as the boy's cries for his parents faded as he disappeared behind closed doors. I was too young to understand why that boy was acting so crazy, but I knew I did not want to be him – to be the next crazy child hauled away from my family forever. I didn't even understand why I was here.

I tugged on my mum's jeans and took a few steps back.

'Mummy, I don't like it here.' I whispered, my voice cracking.

My mum stared down at me, watching as my eyes exploded with tears before finally kneeling down next me. I could only see dirty blonde locks as she messed up my hair. I shook my head to clear my vision only to see her forced smile.

'You don't have to be afraid sweet, ah, Dylan. This place will give you all the adventures you like. You belong here.'

I reached up and gently wiped her eyes. 'I belong with you and Daddy.'

'Not yet, my darling, not yet,' Her voice was monotone as she robotically caressed my face before standing up.

I turned to Dad who also watched the scene with an aloof expression on his face.

'Daddy, please! Please don't leave me here!' I wailed.

'You must serve your purpose, Dylan' he stated flatly.

I was dumbfounded. I could not believe my parents wanted me gone. Tears poured down my face as I turned away from them. Parents are supposed to love their children, not hate them. My hands trembled at my sides, torn between wanting to hug my parents and avoid their touch altogether. I stuffed them into my jacket pockets and stared intently at the ground. Hot tears rolled down my cheeks and past my quivering jaw. *Why did they want me to leave?*

Didn't they love me anymore? Have I done something wrong?

I quickly wiped my eyes and placed my hand back inside my pocket. I vowed never to forgive them.

Even when I found out I was being sent away, there were not many moments I was comforted by my parents. They had always been there for me, but in the last couple of months before my departure, they became cold and aloof, not only to me but also my newborn twin brothers Jeremy and David.

I was upset over not getting attention from my parents. As they continued to ignore me – only giving me the time of day to care for my basic needs – I felt more like a tenant than their child. It seemed as if they didn't know what to do with us. But being with my family and ignored seemed much better than not being with them at all.

'All new students please make your way to the main hall.'

'You need to go now, Dee,' my father said.

I wiped away the new tears forming in my eyes and began to follow the many young students all flooding into the theatre. None of us looked back, not even once.

Inside was fairly normal, except for the large, gothic throne the colour of gold – this was contrasted with its decorations of much darker-coloured symbols and carvings. I stared at the thrown in awe, it seemed to create a quality of beauty in this cold place. On one of its arms was a large red button, which seemed to be getting a great deal of attention. I could hear the whispers of those around me wondering what it could be for.

As I took a seat in the audience, I spotted the young boy from before. I felt sorry for him now and wanted to give him one of the cupcakes in my lunch bag. But he was not upset anymore. He was smiling with an eerily stoic look in his eyes. I shifted uncomfortably in my seat before looking up at the front.

With the click of her annoyingly bright coloured heels, Ms McGuirk – the school principal – walked onto the stage. She wore a dark grey suit. Her bright green hair and matching shoes created a bit of a chuckle among some of the students. She smiled at us all, her eyes dazzling and welcoming as she sat down on the large gold throne. Her hand hovered over the red button before resting upon her lap. The muffled chatter quieted as if on instinct.

'Welcome students!' She smiled, 'Welcome to Albanrouke Academy for the Gifted. This school is like no other and will specially cater for your purpose – so you can become what you truly need or want to be.'

I watched Ms McGuirk intently, and found myself only paying attention to the sound of her sweet voice; although I did not understand the strange language fluttering from her waxy lips. Feeling a bit overwhelmed, I glanced around and saw nearly half the students smiling and nodding along with the principle while others shared my confusion. It would be several months until I was properly conditioned and I fully understood the language used at Albanrouke. And why.

Unsure if I should listen or not, I decided to zone out and think of the good times I had with my family before finding myself following the stream of students out of the hall. They were calling out various names and gave each child a piece of paper before sending them off in a hurry. It was not long before my name was called and I received my small piece of paper. On it was the number of my dorm room. Without a moment to breathe, I was pushed off towards my new home.

Chapter One

Age 17, Inside Albanrouke Academy, 2017

A resounding alarm sounds through the speakers tucked in the corner of every room and every hall in every building of this wretched school. This is how every day begins.

The signal.

Must wake up.

Must get dressed.

I pick out one of seven blue cotton shirts.

Check.

I slip on one of two button-front grey school dresses.

Check.

I walk to a drawer and pull out socks from a neatly formed row of folded, identical pairs and put them on.

Check.

I put on my standard-issue school shoes.

Check.

The alarm is silenced.

First mission of the day: Accomplished.

I'm hungry! When's breakfast?

Be quiet! Be patient.

My bedroom door opens automatically with a loud click. A line of the others, all dressed as I am, are slowly marching along the hallway.

Promptly step in line.

Follow silently. Step by step.

Hushed whispers? That's not allowed. Shh, stay out of trouble.

Keep going.

I smell bacon and eggs, and my stomach begins to grumble.

Keep walking.

There are the same teachers standing watch.

Ignore. Keep walking.

I grab a breakfast tray. A worker places a plate, drink and my tablets on it.

Follow line.

Sit down.

Eat.

As I eat the same meal they serve each morning, the grumbling in my stomach ceases. But I still want more.

"Hi, Dee."

It's Mira. Why is she talking?

Silence.

Take a sip of drink.

"How have you been?" asks Mira.

Stop talking, Mira.

Mira looks directly into my eyes. Her hair is styled differently. And there's something different about her uniform.

Different. Not good.

Mira, what's gotten into you?

My hands begin to shake.

Take a sip of drink.

Mira doesn't seem to notice that I'm nervous or that she's going to get in trouble if she keeps talking and acting outside of protocol. She asks me, "Don't you wish we had more free time?"

Oh, Mira, why are you still talking? Stop.

Have more than a sip.

My hands begin to tremble more intensely. I can't even hold my glass properly. When I try to set it down, I miscalculate the distance to the table. Something falls.

I look down. My tablets are scattered about the floor. I must pick them up before anyone else notices! *Quick, pick them up before I get in trouble!*

Pick up tablets.

The tiles are white; the pills are white. Everything is white. *I can't see my pills! Where are the tablets?*

"Dee. I know this is hard for you to understand. But, I need you to talk to me."

Mira is distracting me from my main objective: finding my tablets. She keeps staring at me. *Why?*

"Dee."

Now, someone is screaming.

Who's screaming?

A boy. Sounds like a boy.

"It's happening again." Dee continues to stare at me while I frantically search on my hands and knees for my scattered pills.

Of course, it is, Mira, of course, it is.

"I've worked it out Dee, and they know it. I'll probably be taken today but don't worry. Everything will be okay.'

A flock of teachers and students surround the boy.

Ignore. Do not look.

He's staring straight at us. They grab at his limbs. And plunge a needle deep into his neck.

Ignore.

Silence. Back to normal. Routine.

An intense, resounding alarm – more like a siren – blasts through the air. I know this warning alarm as well as I the routine schedule alarm.

Obey.

Stand up.

I stand straight, my back away from my friend, Mira.

What about my tablets?

"Dee, stop ignoring me."

Mira, stop talking. You have to stop. It's not needed.

I can sense danger in the air.

Walk away.

"Dee. I'm sorry."

Sorry for what? Talking?

No.

Open communication should be normal. Normal? What's normal?

Follow routine.

This isn't routine.

Keep walking.

I hear more screaming coming from somewhere behind me.

Who is that?

Does not matter. Ignore.

I march with the others to my classroom and get my books. As I pass a large mirror, I glance at my reflection. Everything around me, including me, is clinical and sterile. At the corner of the mirror, I notice something move.

Or did I?

What is that?

Ignore.

Go to class.

Sit down.

Where's Mira? She isn't here. What happened to her? Did they —

Then I see her.

Calm down.

Follow routine.

"Alright everyone, today we will be reviewing the main methods and techniques of systems science."

Listen. Pay attention.

"At first, let us distinguish between the broad patterns which recur amongst complex systems."

Take notes.

Something's wrong.

"Nonetheless, it is not vacuously all embracing; it excludes both systems whose parts just cannot do very much."

Suddenly, Mr Awad becomes silent. He turns to the door, which always locks when class begins. I hear the familiar sound of the latch automatically releasing.

What's happening? Class has only just begun.

My eyes are fixed on the door. So are Mr Awad's and everyone else's. When she walks in, I try not to gasp.

What's she doing here?

Stand up when in her presence.

This can't be good.

I remembered that Mira was a few seconds later to class than everyone else.

Could that be what this is about?

Try to ignore. Follow routine.

"Ms McGuirk?" Mr Awad nervously smiles.

He's always nervous around her. Wait. What?

No. Stop. Pay attention. Follow routine.

"You may sit down," Ms McGuirk says with a calm, even tone.

Sit.

We all sit down in unison, including Mr Awad.

When was her hair pink? It's always changing colour.

Stop. Forget. Pay attention.

"No need to worry, everyone. Just making sure you are all working." Her voice is as honeyed as her yellow, hollow eyes that are narrowing to examine us.

We're always working. Do we do anything else?

No. Stop. Pay attention.

Pay attention to what? Her?

Yes. Must follow routine.

My heart is racing. I try not to shift in my seat or make any movement to show how anxious I am.

Calm down. You've done nothing wrong.

Pay attention.

PAY ATTENTION.

Ms McGuirk then lifts one of her hands, her index finger slowly folding out to point to one of us.

She's pointing? Pointing to whom?

Me?

No. I follow routine.

I follow the invisible line from her fingertip to its target right beside me. Mira.

Mira has been noticed. I have to –

No.

Yes.

Ms McGuirk interrupted my internal battle when she commands, "You. Stand up."

My stomach begins to churn.

Why? I know this isn't good. Don't let this happen.

Mira stands up.

No. This isn't real.

Yes, it is.

"You are ready, Miss Santos. You won't reject it anymore." Ms McGurick straightens up and clasps her hands behind her back.

Reject what?

The change.

What change?

It happens every day.

No. This is crazy.

Stop. Pay attention.

Mira nods.

This needs to stop.

No. It's normal. Routine.

Normal?

Yes, normal. Routine.

Routine?

Yes, routine.

I don't like it.

Stop. Ignore.

I don't want to.

You must.

Mira is walking away. Ms McGurick is following her.

Nobody's stopping it. It has to be stopped.

No. Ignore.

No.

Yes.

I need to –

Shut up.

"Stop!" The word just flies out of my mouth.

Mira stops walking. Ms McGuirk stops walking. The teacher and my classmates are staring at me.

Why are they staring at me?

You talked.

No, I didn't.

Yes. You did. Danger.

Mr Awad clears his throat. "Did you take your medication this morning?"

Well, that's a stupid question. Of course, I did!

Did I?

I try to remember the events of the morning. Something is clouding my head, probably my anxiety from having everyone in class gawking at me. I distinctly recall Mira talking. Out loud. I was nervous for some reason. My hands shook too much to pick up my drink. Then I knocked something to the ground. My tablets. Yes, I remember my pills scattering on the white tiles. But as I tried to collect them, someone began screaming.

The boy from the dining hall was staring straight at us.

Why is everyone always screaming?

Why doesn't Mira scream? Why isn't she fighting back?

"I got distracted," I tell Mr Awad. It's not a lie.

Bad answer. Should have stayed silent.

Run. Get out.

No.

I can't stay here.

Ms McGuirk marches toward me.

No. Follow routine. Routine is safe.

I'm face to face with Ms McGurick. Her upper lip curls as she glowers at me.

Get out now.

No. Trust the program.

Ms McGuirk clenches my lower jaw in her hand. I feel a sharp, stinging sensation as her grip gets tighter and tighter. Her eyes narrow.

Why is this happening?

You remember.

I've forgotten. Forgotten what?

"You stupid little girl," she sneers before flinging me to the side. Ms McGuirk is laughing.

I don't understand why.

"How do you propose you were going to stop this?" She continues mocking me, "That somehow you would be able to protect your *friend*? That she would still reject the change like you still do?" Her sharp eyes scan me up and down.

It takes all my strength to make sure I don't move an inch.

"That's not your order to give."

Orders. Must follow orders. Silence. Be quiet.

But Mira is my friend. I have to do something. What kind of person would I be if I let them take her and change her?

Mira will be back.

She'll be different.

Does it matter?

Yes. It does matter. She matters.

Ms McGuirk releases her grip on my jaw. As she turns away from me, she heaves a sigh thick with disdain and tedium. She then motions to Mira and they make their way to the door. I watch helplessly as they get closer and closer to the exit.

No. I'm not going to let this happen.

I run straight towards them. As I dodge through the chairs and desks, I hear the muffled voices of my classmates. I stop caring about what they think. I have to catch up to Mira. I have to save her.

"Grab her! Quickly!" Mr Awad shouts.

I seize the doorknob and twist it open as fast as I can. Before the automatic lock is reset. My sweaty fingers make it difficult to pull the door open. "Mira!" My voice sounds brittle and disembodied as I shriek her name. I wish I could be sure it's coming from me.

She's right there, obediently following Ms McGuirk. Both of them ignore me.

"Mira! Please turn around!" I plead. "Please talk to me!" I purse my lips together as I hear the teacher call my name. Glancing back to see him and all my classmates standing behind me, I see their sneering faces filled with hatred.

They step closer, moving as if one entity. One mind.

They're everywhere. Surrounding me.

I notice Mr Awad brandishing a thin metallic needle. He skulks toward me with sadness swirling within his dark eyes, his lips set in a straight line as he raises the needle and brings it down.

So sharp. It stings. It won't stop stin –

**

Careful.

Voices morph together. Even from everything I know about what happens here, I still can't understand what they're saying.

'Where's Mira?' I ask openly.

Suspicious eyes stare down at me. How subtle of them.

'Do not worry about her. Mira is absolutely fine. You are the one we need to –' A nurse begins, but I interrupt.

'No, she isn't. Mira isn't fine.'

The doctor clears his throat. 'Did you take your medication yesterday morning?'

'I got distracted.' My icy tone could have frozen water.

'By what?' the doctor asks.

I purse my lips together. 'You already know.'

Wrong answer. Cooperate. Follow routine.

Why did I say that? Why do I keep telling myself to follow the routine? What routine?

Apologize.

No. Let's see what happens.

The doctors and nurses all glance at each other before turning to me once again.

Why are they looking at me with such concern?

'Miss Inarkaevich, we advise that you do not resist,' the nurse stated flatly.

Resist what?

Without warning, hands grasp at my limbs. They are holding me down. I can't move.

The doctor opens my jaw and stuffs tablets down my throat.

Do I swallow? I'm scared. I don't want to swallow them.

Yes, you do.

I try to open my jaw, but he holds it shut.

Resist. Fight back. It's not too late. Fight back.

Too bad.

They're talking again. Do I listen? No, I'm not in class.

Ignore. Listen. Obey.

I hear the tap, tap, tap of heavy heels on linoleum. Somehow, I know it's her. She's back to supervise. I can't see her, but I see the nurses' posture stiffen and straighten.

Good little soldiers.

Pay attention.

'She is highly skilled and is one of our best. Yet, she has not been changed. Why?'

'From her daily scans, it appears her body will still reject it. Even though she is more capable than Mira, we cannot proceed to the next step,' explains the doctor.

Cooperate.

No, I don't want to go back to the way I was.

'If she is not ready by graduation, we will have to force it. As you know, that will involve some catastrophic experiences.' The nurse replies.

Pay attention.

'It will be forced upon her anyway. Especially if she keeps going the way she is. Especially since awakening.' There is a brief pause. 'We should have known she would react like that.'

'She and all other students were trained for this.'

'Yes, but that doesn't mean there will not be problems. And we found our problem.'

'It will be dealt with.'

'Good.'

This doesn't sound right. Can I do anything to stop this?

Ignore.

But it's Ms McGuirk. I have to take notice.

It is over now. Ignore.

Ignore?

Ignore.

Chapter Two

The morning alarm sounds. Another day begins.

The signal.

Must wake up.

Must get dressed.

I pick out one of seven blue cotton shirts.

Check.

I slip on one of two button-front grey school dresses.

Check.

I walk to a drawer and pull out socks from a neatly formed row of folded, identical pairs and put them on.

Check.

I put on my standard-issue school shoes.

Check.

The alarm is silenced.

First mission of the day: Accomplished.

Breakfast?

Breakfast.

My bedroom door opens automatically with a loud click. A line of the others, all dressed as I am, are slowly marching along the hallway. Same as always.

Promptly step in line. Follow silently.

Halt.

She's here again.

'No need to worry, just a routine check-up,' a man's voice shouts.

Routine. Follow routine.

This isn't routine.

Different. Stay calm. Obey.

I stand as still as the others, my eyes staring at the back of the head of the one in front of me. I can hear the methodical, heavy tap, tap, tap of her heels on the linoleum floor while she paces back and forth. Back and forth. She's scanning us.

Stand up straight. Focus.

The hushed whispers of teachers waft over me.

What are they saying? Why are they talking?

Ignore.

Worry lines are plastered across Mr Awad's forehead.

Ignore.

'You may continue.'

Obey. Keep walking.

When the line makes it to the cafeteria, I grab a tray. A woman places a plate, drink and tablets on my tray.

Follow line. Sit. Eat. Follow routine.

Mira sits across from me. We look at each other. Everyone else is looking down at their food. I break eye contact with Mira and continue eating.

Take sip of drink. Do not forget.

Don't forget what?

Do not forget tablets.

I pick up the tablets and place them in my mouth. Then, I grasp my glass and raise it. But I pause just briefly.

Do not forget. Do not forget. Take them. Take them now.

An overwhelming feeling of being watched comes over me.

Who's watching?

Do not worry. Ignore.

I look around, careful only to move my eyes. I see Mira. She's watching me. I dart my eyes away from her penetrating stare.

Concentrate. Focus. Take the tablets.

Placing the drink to my lips, I swallow, careful not to look anywhere but down.

Must follow routine.

Must...

Always....

Follow routine.

An alarm sounds. It's deep and resonates throughout the hall. Breakfast is over, and it's time to go to economics class.

Obey. Stand up. Get books. Go to class. Sit in assigned seat.

Where's Mira?

I quickly glance over and see that Mira is seated in her usual spot right next to me. Nothing has changed.

Stop looking. Focus. Pay attention.

'Recapping our discussion of cost of capital. The cost of debt is the market interest rate that the firm has to pay on its long term borrowing today, net of tax benefits...'

Take notes.

'One approach is to use the regression beta.' Mr Tsao continued.

I can't help myself. I glance at Mira again. She's taking notes just like everyone in the class. They are all clones of each other, with the same notebooks and pens. Even their writing is in sync.

Ignore. Focus.

'Miss Inarkaevich, could you repeat what I just said?'

All eyes turn to me. Simultaneously.

I clear my throat. 'You need taxable income for interest to provide tax savings. Note that the EBIT at Disney is worth $10,032 million.'

Mr Tsao's eyes narrow, 'Good.'

Focus. Pay attention.

**

I'm now in the library for my study period. I begin reading the book 'Unexpected Similarities in the Courtship of Humans.' Several of the others are here too. I notice we are all synchronised.

We all read, turn a page, continue. Read. Turn a page. Continue. Read. Turn a page –

The thing that catches my awareness is the rustle of all the pages turning simultaneously.

That's curious.

Ignore. Focus.

Again, a feeling of being watched engulfs me. I have to find out who it is this time. It's a boy; I don't know him. He's watching me, and Mira's watching him. I see confusion and maybe something else in her eyes. I don't know.

Ignore.

I resume my task of reading and turning the next page in perfect timing with the others.

The sound of a book shutting and shuffling papers distracts me. I carefully look up.

'Are you sure you want to do this, Soren?' Mira smirks, her eyes twinkling with mischief.

Mira and Soren stare at each other for a long moment. Without saying a word, he gets up and walks away. Mira smiles slightly. Then she picks up her book.

Ignore.

I resume reading.

Read. Turn page. Continue.

'Do not get any ideas,' Mira states firmly.

Why is she talking?

She is changed. She is allowed.

I turn to look at her. A fictitious smile lifts her cheeks.

'Ideas about what?' I ask.

I feel like I've done something wrong by replying.

Silence is essential.

Mira tilts her head to the side as if trying to figure me out. I don't even blink. We both look away once again, pick up our books, and begin reading.

Read. Turn Page. Continue.

Take notes.

'Dylan,' Mira states as if naming any inanimate object in the room.

Why does she keep talking to me? Is this a test?

'Do not forget to take your medication.'

I won't forget. Why would I forget?

Mira's eyes glance down towards my pocket.

I take out the container inside and reach for my water bottle.

'You were going to forget again, admit it.' She keeps talking.

I'm going to get noticed. I can't get noticed.

I open the container and take out one of the pills. In just a few seconds, it's flowing down my throat along with some water. I close the container and put it back in my pocket. I'm glad that it's over and soon had my required reading back in my hands.

'Cives inde in Novum Mundum,' Mira says. There's a soft ruffle of papers as Mira stands up. 'Go back to your dorm for now.'

I look straight up at her, confusion apparent in my eyes.

Mira looks down at the textbook in my hands and back at me. 'You can take that with you.'

Mira follows some students leaving class. The room is silent once again. I quickly shut the book and put it inside my bag then get up to leave the room without delay.

Mira said to leave. I need to obey her now, too.

Exactly.

I turn back to my remaining classmates in an attempt to plea for help, but they have all turned away – staring down at their desks. Not knowing what else to do, I exit the classroom.

The hallways are now practically empty. Mira and the others have disappeared around the corner. The sound of my footsteps only fills the silence.

When I hear the creak of a door, I stop walking immediately. I turn around. There is only one door open.

Nobody's there.

Suspicious.

Breathe in. Breathe out. Try to stay calm.

Ignore. Keep walking.

A sudden rush of footsteps confuses and paralyses me. With great force, I'm suddenly yanked into one of the classrooms. The door shuts tight behind me.

Some deep-seated instinct to survive awakens in me. Breaking free of their hold, I elbow someone in the stomach.

I watch him wince slightly, his body moving downward before I ball up my hand into a fist and punch upward into his jaw. Moving fast, I grab his arm and twist it, kicking into the back of his knee cap forcing him to kneel on the ground.

'Dylan, stop!' It is Soren.

I turn around slightly and see a group of four to five people watching. I only recognise Soren.

With just that small distraction, my loosened grip causes the guy beneath me to swing at my feet.

As I feel gravity slowly pull me to the ground, a hand grabs at my back. The world spins, and I hit the floor with a painful thud.

I'm aware of hushed whispers.

I shouldn't be here. I need to leave.

I quickly jump to my feet.

'Dylan, we need you to listen,' Soren says.

More soft mumbles surround me. I can just make out some words involving 'Mira' and 'trust.'

They really shouldn't be talking.

Silence is essential.

The guy I had just fought with steps forward. He's awfully bruised. I smirk slightly at what I managed to do.

'I'm Mohamed. Want to sit down?' he asks.

I follow his pointed finger to a nearby chair and back again. My defiant stare is my answer.

'Okay then,' he says.

A tall girl steps forward. 'Mira told us a lot about you before she, ah, she changed. Did she tell you anything about us?'

Mira talks too much.

Mira is allowed to talk now. These people are not allowed.

'That day, you know, when you tried to save her. Why?' the girl asks.

'Dylan forgot to take her medication, Danielle,' Mohamed mumbles.

'That's not the point,' she snaps.

There's a brief pause.

'Dylan,' Danielle begins, 'Since, ah, since Mira spoke so highly of you, we want you to join us.'

Tell Mira. She will report to Ms McGuirk.

I take a couple of steps back.

'No, Dylan, don't leave!' Soren exclaims. 'We'll tell you everything in time, but right now, you need to stay here.'

Danielle takes a small piece of paper out of her pocket and gives it to Soren. He reads over it before handing it back.

'Give that to the dorm head,' Soren tells Danielle before turning to me once again. 'This note is signed by both Mr Awad and the school nurse and relays that you're sick and can't be in class for the next few days. Dylan, we're going to get the drug completely out of your system.'

Who are these people? Why are they doing this? Should I trust them?

Danger. Report.

Danielle is heading toward the door. These people are all looking at me as if I'm just supposed to believe them when they attacked me and forced me into this room. I need to decide what to do. And quickly. I could follow behind Danielle and get into the hall. Then run.

Oh, no! She is already at the door.

I dash towards the door.

'Quick! She's trying to escape!'

With the sound of a door locking shut, they all grab my limbs and carry me towards a large chair at the back of the room. I scratch them with my nails and try to move my restrained arms in attempts to hit them. But they don't stop. In just a couple of seconds, I am tied down to the chair.

'We know you don't want to now, but you're going to help us,' Mohamed's voice is calm as he takes out a needle and plunges it into my arm.

Another needle? Why is it always needles?

Chapter Three

An odd silence welcomes me as I awaken from my drug-induced slumber. The first thing I notice is long, blackened timber boards above me; they have taken me somewhere else. *How long have I been asleep?*

In an instant, I'm alert. I swing my feet off the chair and rest them upon the dirt floor. My heart beats loudly within my chest, and my palms sweat so much that I can't get a proper grip on the door handle. It takes me a couple of seconds to realise that the door is locked. *What's wrong with me?* I should have already known it would be locked. I shouldn't have even bothered trying to open it.

Glancing at my digital watch, I can see it is late in the afternoon. I know that everyone should still be in class. *But where am I?* I need to find out. Bunching up my annoyingly long skirt in my hands, I part my legs and ready myself to kick the door open.

Breathe in. Breathe out.

Slowly I raise my foot, making sure it's in line with the lock. With as much strength as I can muster, I close my eyes and kick forward. But instead of the door, the ball of my foot comes in contact with somebody's stomach.

Mohamed doubles over and clutches his stomach in pain. 'God, you're ruthless,' he chuckles.

I raise my fists. 'Get out of my way.'

He steps backwards and closes the door behind him, 'Sorry, but we need to explain everything to you and introduce you to Ruby and Faruz.'

'I'm not interested.'

I can't forget any of this because I need to tell Mira. I scrutinise him carefully. He has olive skin, light brown eyes and very short dark brown hair. I have to guess his height (about 4'8"), and he's slightly overweight. *How can he be overweight with our training regimine?*

'Are you checking me out?' Mohamed asks with a smirk.

He looks older than he is. He should be easy to get past, especially since he should be weakened from yesterday. *Was it yesterday that they forced me into that room?*

'Not in the way you're thinking of.' I reply, crossing my arms in front of my chest.

He trudges past me and sits in one of the many empty seats surrounding us. With a large stretch, he relaxes completely into the seat.

This is too easy.

'You should sit down. Everyone will be here soon enough.' He pauses. 'You've met Ruby and Faruz already. They're the ones who tied you down in the first place. But, they didn't introduce themselves like the rest of us. You didn't even notice, did you?'

I turn away from him, 'I noticed what I needed to.'

'And you're noticing me now. Who are you going to tell? Mira. Nope. She'll know you're not drugged anymore straight away. Just opening your mouth to talk to her will give you away. So, Dylan, what are you going to do?'

What will I do? 'She's my friend, she'll understand.'

'Yes, she will be grateful that you ratted us out, but her only priority is to serve Ms McGuirk. We'll all be killed. And not just us. You too. She's not your friend.'

I don't want to listen to him. What he's saying doesn't make any sense. *I can't believe any of them. I need to tell Mira.* 'What are you going to do? Beat me up again? It won't be as easy this time.' *His confidence in his abilities will be his downfall.* We were in the same Martial Arts Practical, so I know his fighting patterns.

The click of the door opening pricks my ears. I quickly back behind the chairs. *Who will it be this time?*

The door swings open and Soren appears. He sits down next to Mohamed.

I need to leave. I need to get back to my dorm.

'Good to see that you're up,' Soren smiles at me.

'She's still very aggressive,' Mohamed mumbles. 'I'd keep my distance.'

Soren nods, his forehead creasing, probably thinking of what to do next. I look at the door and then at him. Now, it's two of them against one of me. Soren seems to be around 6'0", fair skin, black eyes, and dark brown hair. He seems to be the obvious leader. Escaping from this group might be harder now, especially because I keep hesitating. *What's stopping me from leaving? I could have gone by now.* I inch my way towards the door.

'Where is everyone else?' Mohamed asks.

Soren shakes his head and leans against the wall, 'They're not coming.'

'I thought they were.'

'Too risky. Right, Dylan?'

Well, Soren seems to have a brain. I glance towards the door once again as he says my name.

I pause and turn around to face them. 'You said you would tell me why you did this to me. Why don't you explain yourselves?'

'Isn't it obvious? You won't believe us.' Soren replied.

I fold my arms across my chest. 'I'm glad you realise that.'

'But you will eventually believe us.'

I shake my head and open the door. Just behind me, I can hear Mohamed tell me to keep a straight face. When the door closes behind me, I find that I am standing at the back of the courtyard of Albanrouke Academy. The silence of the school surprises me, and only now I realise that nobody ever comes outside. Thick bars cover every window. I can see students inside not even casting a glance towards me.

The entire place screams: I AM FULL OF SECRETS!

I quickly jog across the pavement and open the door to the main hallway. Everyone stares blankly straight ahead. From time to time, those who were turned have silent conversations passing between them. This only seems to last a couple of seconds before they continue dutifully to their destination.

Keep a straight face. Whatever you do, show no emotion. It's the only way to blend in.

Putting a poker face on, I begin my facade and walk past the others students in the hallway. I can feel my erratic heart beat as I try to stay in control of the speed of my footsteps. I desperately want to get to my dorm. I want to be alone.

Faces begin to blur; my breathing accelerates. I can feel sweat starting to drip down my temples as I near the dorms. The never-ending silence around me only makes me feel unsafe. I can easily be noticed. Just one mistake and...

I quickly grip my doorknob and twist it. In just a couple of seconds, I have the door shut tightly behind me. Only then can I release a giant sigh of relief. *I made it.*

'It's going to be a bit hard to adjust to everything, but it gets better.'

I jump slightly. Mrs Kangas is sitting on my bed. Her light brown eyes stare at me with a strange sort of sympathy. She isn't in her nurse uniform but is wearing very stylish, neutral-coloured clothes. Her straight white hair is worn down rather than in a tight bun. I can't tell her age, but I immediately recognise her. She was there when I was being drugged after what happened with Mira.

'Why are you–' I begin.

'There's no need to worry about that,' she states softly but firmly. 'What you need to worry about is how to avoid taking your meds. Mira is keeping an eye on you, so it's going to be hard.'

As soon as I had met Soren and his gang, I knew things would be difficult. Being under such careful watch by Mira is obviously going to make things a hundred times harder. Stating the obvious is not going to matter; it doesn't help with the solution. I don't want to be part of this, and I definitely don't want to be drugged again.

I nod. 'I'll work it out.'

Mrs Kangas' eyes harden. 'You're not going to survive alone.'

'I want to see everything for myself before I help. I still have too many unanswered questions.'

Mrs Kangas stands up and walks towards me. Her voice has an urgency to it when she tells me, 'Questions. Answers. It's all wasting time. Mira will have –'

'I don't care.' I shake my head violently, like a child having a tantrum.

Mrs Kangas sighed. 'Didn't you notice your surroundings as you came here? Didn't you hear the silence? See the blank faces of your classmates? Notice how clean and white this place is? It's obvious that something strange is happening. Just because you're being forced into this doesn't mean you can't already see what is going on around you.'

My heart beats furiously within my chest, and I struggle to remain calm as she crosses her arms and stares at me with penetrating eyes. *She doesn't trust me, and I sure don't trust her.* 'I see how people act around here, but I don't understand why. I want to know what I'm fighting against...who I'm fighting against. Before I agree to anything, I want to know what I'm getting myself into.'

Mrs Kangas shakes her head and places her hands upon my shoulders. 'Dylan, you're already part of this.' She takes her hands and straightens her jacket. 'The thing is, nobody knows what we're fighting against. That's what we're trying to find out.'

'Okay, but I'm not just going to join in. I don't trust any of you. At least, not yet. This could all be a trick. Give me time.'

Mrs Kangas sighs again, 'Fine, but please trust me on this. After a day, maybe even just an hour, your decision is going to be a very one.' She side-steps me and opens my door. 'Have you got a plan to deal with your meds?'

'No.' I lie.

'Well, that's something you should start thinking about. I'll talk to you again soon.'

She immediately disappears behind the door and locks it. Locking the door is routine, and I would've locked the door myself if she hadn't, just to keep up appearances. I don't trust what either she or Soren had told me, but I know to truly understand the situation I have to be off the medication. It seems to be controlling me, making me obedient and making me oblivious to what is happening around me. What I need to do is come up with an idea to make Mira think that I'm taking my tablets. Everything after that is simple.

My plan isn't fancy, but I think it will work. I need a plastic pocket liner for my jacket. I'll put a small amount of water in it, just enough to dissolve my daily tablets when I drop them the pocket rather than my mouth. The trick will be getting the pills inside the pocket under Mira's watchful eyes. I really don't want to believe that Mira has been turned. We have always been alike – did nearly everything together since we met at the academy – and it's strange to think how different we've become. We're now polar opposites with different dreams and motives, one more sinister than the other. I had trusted her, but now that has all changed. I wish they had taken me, instead. She didn't deserve to have her life snatched away. I suppose none of us did.

Right now, the plastic pockets I need are full of my class notes. They lay on top of the massive pile of textbooks and modules on my desk. A groan escapes my lips as I realise that I will have a lot of homework to catch up on. But I'm a procrastinator, so it's an easy decision: I'll worry about it later. Without further thought, I grab the plastic pockets and empty them. As I place my notes within my draws, I grab a pair of scissors and cut them to a size that fits inside my pockets. I'm surprised by how much my hands are shaking. The quivering sensation travels from my fingertips to my heart, which is beating restlessly. *If I can just clear my head of these drugs, maybe I can find out what's happening for myself – maybe I could just make my own decisions...*

Thirty minutes later, my 'tablet disposal' system is finished. Then I realise there are two problems.

One, the water might spill out.

Two, I still haven't worked out how to trick Mira.

I don't want to admit it, but I am afraid.

Chapter Four

My heart speed increases the closer I get to the cafeteria. The sterile environment emphasises how much of an outsider I feel – a weakling, a parasite – and that at any moment I could be found out. I can feel the water swishing around in the plastic bag through the thin layer of my skirt material. I had only put a little water in, but still, I'm paranoid. And I have every right to be.

Following the silent footsteps of my classmates, I walk into line and receive a tray from a cafeteria worker with a bowl of porridge, glass of water, spoon and, lastly, my medication. Looking straight ahead, I hope I'm the only one who notices my erratic, panicky pulse. I still don't know if I'll succeed, and I hope that my nervousness – like an annoying itch – will just go away.

Mira is already eating her breakfast by the time I get there. I use brief eye contact to establish my greeting before I sit down and begin my meal. I can tell she's watching me as I take my first spoonful of porridge, and the only thoughts that cross my mind are negative. Each one increases my worry and makes me feel as if I am destined to fail. I'm convinced that all the emotions I'm trying to hide are displayed all over my face. *I'm dwelling too much on my thoughts. They're not facts; they're just thoughts passing by. I need to focus on the task at hand. But then, that's the whole issue, isn't it?*

Because Mira had been changed, or turned, like the others, her awareness will be keen. Every hour, she will leave with everyone else to report back to whoever is in control. At least that's my guess. So, if I don't do this right, I'm going to be hauled away once again. There has to be a way to distract her momentarily.

But only now I realise that it's already too late. She's part of Soren's group. She knows their plans; she's the one who recommended me. It's only a matter of time until –

'Dylan.'

My eyes shoot up.

'Start running,' Mira says firmly.

Don't react. She's testing me.

Fighting the urge to reply, I take another bite of my breakfast. I can feel Mira's eyes on me as I begin to reach for my tablet.

She licks her lips and slowly leans towards me over the table. 'You should be more careful,' she whispers.

I slowly meet her eyes.

A smirk is tugging at her lips.

She's waiting for me to react. She knew this whole time! But where are the others?

I can feel sweat slowly building up on my skin as I struggle to find a way to get out of this situation. *If I run, where to? And how can I warn the others?*

Mira tilts her head to the side, watching me with amusement twinkling in her eyes. The act of watching her begins to hurt my eyes, and my heart still threatens to burst out of my chest. The glass of water is right in front of me and begins to ripple as if mocking me. It ripples again, and suddenly the whole room begins to shake.

Everybody stops eating and stares blankly into the space in front of them. I attempt not to freak out when a bright light suddenly comes through the barred windows. I wince from the light as an incredibly loud noise sends a shockwave through the school. The windows shatter and broken glass cascades to the floor. Still, nobody moves.

I do my best to follow their example when I see Danielle sprint from her chair to the nearest window.

'They blew it up! Soren, we're –'

I want to stop her. I want her to shut up. I wish she hadn't gotten out of her seat in the first place. Mira giggles and both my drugged classmates and the changed ones all turn their heads to the panicked Danielle.

My lip quivers as everyone slowly stands up and walks towards her. Mira watches me as I stay seated, her smile proud as she looks back at Danielle who is now fighting our classmates with ease. But there are too many. *She's going to lose.*

Mira gets out of her seat and walks around the table. She leans in closely to my ear. 'You know, you two were the only ones who bothered to come to breakfast? Where could the others be? I could tell you, but it's already too late.'

I push her back and stand up, my chair toppling as I run out into the hallway. I can hear Danielle screaming from back inside the cafeteria. As I frantically run through the hallways, I realise I don't know where I'm going. I just need to get away.

Every now and again, the sounds of screaming slice the silence like a knife. I shudder from the sounds echoing around the building. *I should have gone to help them, whoever was screaming...even if it was that group. No one deserves to suffer.* I hadn't seen Soren in the cafeteria, so maybe he escaped. But maybe he hadn't. I don't want to think about that.

In front of me, I can see the door to the courtyard; it has been blown open by the blast and hangs from the hinges like a thin piece of paper. As I get nearer, I can see the debris from he shack across the grass, and I wonder how none of it came inside. A thick layer of dust covers just outside the door. Ignoring every instinct saying that I should stay inside, I take a deep breath and run out of the courtyard.

The dust fills my lungs, and my body splutters in attempt to clear my airways. It isn't long until the dust begins to settle and I can see someone standing in front of the now-destroyed shack. Whoever it is, the person has obviously heard me; their lips move rapidly as f barking out commands. In a couple of seconds, more bodies appear. They stand on the outskirts of the courtyard, just watching. *All of this just for one person?*

Surveying what is around me, a glinting silver metal catches my eye. I turn my head to look at it carefully and see that it's a small gate. Dust has settled on it, but it somehow still stands strong. It rattles slightly against the breeze until, suddenly, it opens. Parting my feet in preparation, I take one last glance to the faces around me and sprint towards it. My breathing is heavy, and I can hear my heartbeat in my ears. The grass turns to gravel as I approach the gate, small stones getting into my shoes and making it even harder to run in my annoyingly long skirt.

Another couple of steps and I'm there.

But they advance on me. I think I can fight back (and try), but in a matter of seconds they're holding me down. I don't have the strength to struggle against them. *Too many to them.*

'Take her inside,' Ms McGuirk instructs.

They push down my arms and dig their nails into my flesh, causing me to wince in pain. This seems to amuse them. Before I can even cry out, they pull me up and drag me back inside. My feet drag along the tiled floor as they march through the hallway and into the same theatre that I was in when I first came to this forsaken place. Everything is the same, right down to the large throne and the red button on its arm.

With a sudden kick into the back of my knees, I hit the floor. As I begin to get back up, someone shoves a strange metallic device on my head. Two golden bars bolted together are positioned tightly against my skull. I can see Mira watching from the doorway, a small smile tugging at the end of her lips. Then Ms McGuirk saunters in front of me and sits down on the throne.

How fitting.

She smiles and gives a look to one of the teachers nearby, who pulls out two thin, silver rods. My mouth goes dry as he slowly walks towards me, his eyes glinting with smugness as he stares down at me and grabs my head.

Slowly, he raises the rods.

I shut my eyes tight, thinking that he's going to poke me in the eye when I feel the cold metal against my temples. There must be two holes in the device.

Slowly, the pressure from the rods increases.

He lets out a chuckle as I try to pull away, the sharp tips of the rods digging into my flesh. All the while, Ms McGuirk's fingertips continuously trail over the red button.

I can't see a way out of this. If I attack her and wrestle my way out of her grip, the others surrounding me would surely ambush me. *Who knows what would happen to me?*

Escape isn't easy.

Ms McGuirk presses the button.

My temples burn, and I can't help screaming. Tears flow down my cheeks. It won't stop. It won't stop. *Make it stop!*

Breathe in. Breathe out.

Lights are flashing. I don't know what it means. Something deep down inside of me shouts at me to resist. An inner voice tells me that I have the strength to resist whatever they try to do to me.

Breathe in. Breathe out.

I grab one of the rods and pull it. The lights flash again.

I hear shrieks of pain.

It's not me. I stabbed the teacher in the knee.

Breathe in. Breathe out.

A loud alarm sounds. It's the signal used for emergencies, not to tell us when to go to class or wake up. They're worried.

Good.

Chaos. Feet rushing. Arms grabbing. The lights flashed again.

Ignore the confusion. Run.

Pounding footsteps. *Mine? Theirs? Both?*

I'm running away from the theatre and trying to find my out of the building. My breathing is short and uneven. I can hear shouting and screaming behind me. Or is it all around me? It's so hard to tell.

A flash of silver startles me. Large gardening shears arch toward me. I jump. My attacker is thwarted. This time.

Keep running.

I'm outside. I run through the courtyard and to the gate where they caught me before.

This time, I make it. I push through the gate.

I do it. I escape.

Breathe in. Breathe out.

The gate slams shut behind me.

Pain. So much pain. So much blood.

I turn around, expecting to see angry faces.

Breathe in. Breathe out. When will the pain go away?

My head throbs.

It's too much. Just too much...

Chapter Five

Albanrouke's halls filled with a strange grey mist seeping into the corners of the walls and underneath doorways, consuming everything in its path. Nobody ran. Everyone's faces were blank as they walked in two straight lines – not even fazed by the potential danger. I glanced over at Mira, who was walking in the opposite line. She had just begun to smile before the mist concealed her face.

I took a step to the side of the line, the faces blurring amidst each other as they filled the gap I had just emptied. The sound of a crying child filled the deafening silence.

'Hello?' I called out.

'Why are you leaving me?' the voice wailed.

'Where are you?' I called.

My eyes scanned the hall, searching for the distressed child, but I could only see a sea of blurring faces around me. Swirling. Faster and faster.

My eyes suddenly cast down.

'Please don't leave me.' I barely recognised myself as a child: red cheeks, sunken eyes. She reached out to take my hand, her eyes brimming with tears.

'What's going on?' I asked her.

'Don't you love me anymore?' The child screamed her question.

Something knotted up inside me, and I sunk down to my knees. Her small hands still within mine, we stared eye to eye.

'Please don't make me go! Please! Don't you and Daddy love me anymore?'

Tears seeped down her face; tears escaped from my eyes, too. I reached to her in an attempt to wipe them away.

'Dylan?' My voice caught in my throat. 'Dylan?'

She was gone. I searched frantically for those sad eyes, stepping through the haze around me. Two faces lit up, but in a flash, they were gone.

Suddenly, I was sitting on the floor alone. The hall began to darken considerably. The only light left on flickered as I felt eyes on me.

I didn't want to look up, but the sound of shuffling feet caught my attention. Standing in front of me was my parents. Their eyes were colourless, and their faces were devoid of expression. Mum was holding young Dylan's hand, and Dad held a pram firmly in his grip; the sun hood was closed, concealing the babies from view.

'Jerome and David,' I whispered.

I looked back at the younger version of myself. Her eyes were still red and swollen with tears. I watched as my parents loosened the grip on her hand, and (not long after) they let go of the pram. It was only a matter of seconds when they stepped back, and their faces disappeared into the darkness.

A strange beeping sound filled my ears.

'Mummy! Daddy!' The younger me cried out.

Young Dylan cried as she neared the pram, the two babies' own cries echoing throughout the hallway.

'Wait! Please! Don't leave me again!' I choked on my tears. 'I don't want to be alone!'

I clenched my teeth as tears flowed down my face.

'Please...please don't leave...' I muttered, lowering my head.

I shot up, covered in sweat and tears. My throat was dry and the cries of my brothers and younger self were still ringing in my ears. I flung the bed covers off me and sat up. What had I just experienced? It seemed to be like what I studied in psychology last year: dreams.

Did I actually dream? We're not supposed to dream. But was it telling me that I needed to save myself and my brothers?

Wiping my tears, I tried to ignore the images of the dream flashing in my mind. I scanned my surroundings, and it appeared that I was in a sterile room unlike the one at the academy. Beside me was an IV, which was hooked up to my right arm. Nearby was what I only could describe as an armchair. Its material was shiny and metallic, but the chair was inexplicably transparent. It was not (or did not appear to be) truly solid. Across from me was a large painting of a sunflower, creating a sense of reality in the bare room. On the left wall was a small mirror.

As my confusion settled, I remember what had happened. Flashes of metal pierced my memory like a jagged bolt of lightning slicing a stormy sky. The image caused me to immediately grab at my head. I expected to feel the cold metal of the device they placed on me, but I only felt my hair. I could swear that I still felt the cold metal wrapped around my head, but now it was only just a disturbing memory. I wondered if my brothers would experience this pain someday. I hoped that they wouldn't be entering their teens years drugged and being readied for 'slaughter.'

Did my parents leave them as they left me? Are they okay? I need to find them before it's too late.

I took a deep breath and inspected the IV. There was nothing on it to indicate what concoction was being pumped into me. I quickly unhooked myself so I could stop the mystery potion being pumped into me and so that I could get out of this place. I needed to find out where I was. There was a stinging sensation on the wound as some blood seeped through the incision. I shook my hand a bit to lessen the pain. As I reached to open the door, I was surprised to find that it was unlocked. Skeptical, I kept wondering if I should step out into the strangely empty hallway. Images of blurred faces flashed in my mind again, and I was reluctant to step through. But hesitating wouldn't help my brothers.

As I passed the doorway, my ears popped as they do during significant altitude changes. Suddenly, I was surrounded. Everyone around me appeared normal until I noticed a faint glow emanating from their skin. Golden hues and fire-like waves radiated from each of them. I felt the need to retreat to where I had come from. After rubbing my eyes a few times, I noticed that the glow faded from their skin, creating a normal appearance yet again.

This is very strange.

I tapped someone passing by on the shoulder, and asked, "Where am I?"

"What are you talking about?' He asked, his eyes narrowing with suspicion. 'Oh, it is you. I guess the Plutocratic Collective wants to see you. I will take you there.'

'The what?'

'Come on,' he said, ignoring me.

'No. I'm not going anywhere with you. Where's the exit?'

'You do not need to know that.'

'Yes, I do.' I tried to make my voice sound more confident than I felt.

Wisps of golden light began to emanate from his skin as his face darkened with annoyance. He grabbed my arm, the glow becoming more intense.

'Let go of me.' I tried to tug my arm away. I couldn't.

Just as I curled my fingers into a fist to punch him, the light became blinding, and I felt myself being catapulted through the building. His grip still firmly on my arm, I knew he was the one pulling me. Suddenly, I was standing in a large, sleek, platinised panel with an almost invisible line running down the middle.

I took a step back.

'Do not even try,' he said, pulling me back.

A burst of air was released when doors opened (at least, I now believe they were doors). My hair was infuriatingly flying about, covering my eyes and entering my gaping mouth. What's-his-Name was unfazed and led me through the open doors. I nearly fell over from the orce but was kept strangely steady by his grip. In a matter of seconds, the wind died out, leaving me standing there with messy hair and unkempt school uniform on the macadamized floor.

He let go of my arm, his glow fading. I immediately pulled away, rubbing my sore wrist as I glanced about the room. It was empty. Completely empty. If it weren't for the very real pain I still felt from the IV wound, I would have thought I was still dreaming.

Two large cubes suddenly rose from the floor and moved towards me. They scraped along the floor, creating an ear-splitting racket. I was sure there were going to be abrasions left behind them, but there were none.

Amazing.

The din and the cubes stopped only just a few feet in front of me.

Sounds of footsteps approaching made my stomach flip. When I heard my name, I finally looked up to see two figures staring down at me from the top of the cube-like structure. The woman clasped her bronze hands together, preparing herself for what was to come. A couple of seconds later, she flicked some of her wispy, dark-brown hair out of her face, revealing her uninterested hazel eyes. The man was her opposite. He straightened his back and gazed at me sternly, his dark-green eyes striking against his pale skin. I could sense that he was unsympathetic to my very existence within the room. Their eyes watched me as I watched them, each of us calculating the other's motives and possible actions.

'Would you care to look outside?' the woman asked.

The right wall slid upwards and concealed itself within the ceiling as a vivid orange hue caressed our faces. Two large balls of fire hung in the sky, spreading light and draining life from the already dead desert. Large cracks across its surface and what appeared to be melted structures were scattered everywhere. The landscape looked scorched and uninhabitable.

In the corner of my vision, I saw what appeared to be a half-demolished brick wall. A group of people stood beside it and, as if not feeling the heat at all, they were huddled around a small fire. As I stared at the small group, I noticed one of them was playing the violin. Its melancholic melody played inside my mind without ever physically hearing it.

'Where am I?' I asked.

What's-his-Name was suddenly gone from sight. I was standing alone with the two older strangers.

'Can you not recognise your own planet?' I could not recognise the voice who spoke; it was not distinctly male or female.

My breath caught in my throat. After what seemed to be a long silence, I asked, 'What do you mean?'

'This is earth, your future – 80 years in the future.'

Full of shock and suspicion, I chose my words carefully. 'Earth is unrecognisable from its past.'

'Much has changed over the years.'

I stared at the strange landscape in silent disbelief. *This was the future?*

The sound of leather hitting the surface of the cube brought my attention back to the man. In front of him was a leather-bound journal, his eyes wide and steady as he slid it towards me.

'Before you do anything,' he began, 'you should read this. It is a journal written by the Albanrouke Academy officials. All institutions documented their progress, and this is one of those records. You should see what ends up happening to you. Everything has been described in the book. Page by page. Word by word. Nothing has changed for you. We know what your intentions are and we ask that leave immediately.'

'And go where? I don't even know where I am.'

'Back to the past. It is where you belong.'

My skin crawled with disgust as I thought of the place I had been kept for the past twelve years. I didn't want to go back. Anywhere would be better than going back there. 'Why should I?' I asked, trying to keep my voice from wavering.

'Everything you hope to achieve while here changes nothing. There is nothing you can do, so you might as well accept your fate and return right now.'

'Everything I hope to achieve? I haven't had any thoughts like that whatsoever.'

'So far.' He paused. 'Look, it makes no difference. When you read this journal, you will find out anyway. You will understand.'

'And if I don't understand? And if I try to change things? What will happen then?'

'Nothing, everything will remain the same. It will just take longer than the predicted amount of time to get there.'

'How are you so certain?' I sigh.

'Because this is the future.' His jaw clenched slightly with agitation.

I picked up the journal and flipped through its yellowing pages. I remembered Mira, who had been changed. I remembered Soren. I remembered Mohamed and poor Danielle who had lost control of her emotions and been attacked. I didn't like what was becoming of the people I had met. And the future was not fixed. *It couldn't be! Things can change.*

I doubted I could change everything, but maybe I could save someone's life. My two brothers came to my mind again. I hadn't seen them since I was young, but maybe I could go back and…and…what?

'I'll read the book,' I said, 'but I won't promise anything.'

'Your promises are irrelevant.'

I bit my lip, fighting back the need to spout off a few unmentionable words, and then left the room. What's-his-Name was waiting outside.

'So?' I said.

"So?' his strange eyes questioned me.

'So where can I go to read this thing?' I said, holding up the book.

'Careful, do you know how old that is?'

'Eighty years. Now, where can I go to read it?'

'Come with me.'

'Not if you're going to do that weird thing you did on the way here. I'm not going through that again.'

He stepped forward, his gaze forceful as he stared down at me, 'You should be grateful we did not leave you out there for the others to find. Believe it or not, we are the closest to your kind. Many have mutated and changed. They would hardly be any more welcoming.'

I stepped forward and stared straight up at him, 'I'm not the one with the problem, you are. So, why don't you put your attitude away and actually answer my question?'

He shook his head and chuckled, 'You have been drugged for so long that you are emotionless. Sooner or later, it is going to all come back, and you will not be able to handle it.'

'Don't tell me how I'm going to feel. Everything may be unknown to me right now, but I can control myself.'

'Control yourself? You cannot even control your mouth.' He paused. 'Can you even remember what it was like before Albanrouke?' His eyes softened slightly from sympathy for what I believed was never knowing my family and never knowing what the world was really like. Everyone seemed to know everything about me, especially about my failures to come.

'Stop looking at me like that. I don't need your sympathy, so get over whatever emotional issues you have and tell me where I can go to read this thing. Uninterrupted.'

'That is not the problem,' he stated.

'Then I'll just ask someone else.'

'You cannot.'

'Why not?' I challenged.

'It could disrupt –'

'Haven't you heard?' My voice cracked. 'Um, everything is the same in the end.' Even with those words echoing in my head, I still wanted to change it.

'Then why are you still here fighting with me when you already know you are going to fail?'

'Because things *can* change.'

We stared at each other with questioning eyes, full of both stubbornness and worry. We both were trying to work out the other's intentions, and we both did not trust each other. It felt like a long time had passed before he opened his mouth.

He sighed. 'You will just have to learn the hard way,' he said. 'Come on, I might as well take you back to where you woke up.'

'You're not going –'

He grabbed my arm, and in an instant, I was back in that strange hallway. I glanced around to see others walking around us. They didn't seem to care. As I clutched the journal to my chest, I wondered if maybe this could all be some weird dream. *Why couldn't it?* When people have their personalities changed like Mira's was – couldn't they be trapped in a delusion within their minds to keep them from fighting back? Could it be the same for me? This could all just disappear if I woke up.

'I will come back later and see what you have decided,' he smiled.

'But you already know, don't you?' I lowered my eyes, blinking away fresh tears.

'We like to be present in the situation, not just watch it as it unfolds like reading it in the pages.'

'Okay...' My voice wobbled slightly, I bit my lip.

'I am Axon, by the way.'

'Okay,' I repeated.

'I will see you later.'

I turned around and entered the room. Again, I was surrounded by the strange furniture that I first opened my eyes to. Without any time to waste, I sat down on the bed and flicked to the chapter entitled 'Problems'. It was a guess, but I thought it made the most sense to start there.

A couple of pages in, there were three photographs: two of the same young twin boys and one appeared to be a photo of me. The boys had their dirty blonde hair swept to the side and sitting in a rigid posture, their grey eyes staring blankly at the camera. The picture of myself was the same: my hair was tied back, and my eyes stared blankly forward, full of defeat with glints of sadness (of what could have been, I imagined). Each picture was labelled with my name and the names of my twin brothers, Jeremy and David. They would be eleven years old now.

I shivered. I couldn't stop staring at the eyes. With a nervous hand, I turned the page and began to read:

Experiment Number: 10147858
Date: 29/7/2016
Prepared By: Khrele Uavoo

On August 29th, 2016, at approximately 8:15 am, Miss Dylan Inarkaevich sat down for breakfast with Miss Mira Kearney. Miss Kearney had shown signs of drug withdrawal for three weeks, along with a small number of individuals. We continued to watch them closely when Miss Kearney had caused Miss Inarkaevich to drop her medication and begin her own withdrawal process. We had noted that too many students were being taken by this Rebel group and had decided to make an example of Miss Kearney. At roughly 9:40 am, Miss Kearney was chosen by Ms McGuirk to be inserted with the

Hundreds of words detailed my reaction to Mira and how I was slowly being pulled into the group that was led by Soren. It continued to state how I stayed in the future for months, recruiting people for my cause. But no one from the future joins me because they didn't want to erase their own existence. It was understandable, but if they wanted to live why, would they help me in the first place?

The words describing my attempt to fight Ms McGuirk and save my brothers began to fade until there was nothing left but blank pages. But it was obvious that I failed. And yet, I still wanted to change what appeared to be the inevitable. I wanted to try.

If I don't do what the book says I do, maybe it could work.

I felt guilty about how many people I drew into my fight, how much pain I put everyone in and still failed. *Why should I even bother?* I knew why. I had hope. I didn't like seeing what earth had become. I couldn't even recognise where I was. There had to be a way to avoid this disastrous future for my brothers, myself, and the planet.

I just need to get back. I need to find my brothers. I'll find a way to fix things.

During school hours, the dorm rooms were always unlocked. I could wait inside until either Jeremy or David came back from class. I'd be locked inside with one of them until dinner. Then, when the rooms were unlocked and the halls were clear, no, that won't work. My other brother would still be in the cafeteria, amongst the others. I'd have to quickly push him out of his dorm and pull him towards his twin's room. Hopefully, I'd make it in time for all three of us to be in the one dorm room together.

We would have to wait until the dinner alarm was raised and the rooms were unlocked. Three hours would have passed, and I'd have to wait until the halls were clear. Hopefully, that's when we would get out of the academy. With any luck, we'd be fast enough.

'Back already?' I asked, hearing the sounds of footsteps outside the door.

The door opened slightly, and Axon's lime green eyes peeped through, 'How did you know?'

'The sound of your footsteps.' I paused when I heard a small giggle. 'Who's with you?'

His eyes widened a bit with worry, and he closed the door again. I couldn't help but feel surprised by the sudden change in his personality. When we first met, he acted cold and authoritative; now, that facade seemed to be falling, creating a sense of playfulness I had only briefly seen when he told me his name.

How much time had passed? It only seemed about half an hour. Did he already trust me? Or is this another way to cover things up?

And there was a lot to cover up. Flicking through the other chapters, I came across things I would have never believed in and I still refuse to believe. Even with all these future 'people' with the same hair and eye colour as each other, it doesn't mean it's real.

The door flung open and revealed Axon with a very peculiar-looking girl. He stared at her with amused annoyance. She stared at me with the brightest smile I've ever seen. When she squealed slightly, it only added to the strange way she looked.

She had extensive ridges on her nose and small silver eyes. Her hair was a dingy yellow before suddenly deepening in colour and becoming a bright orange, contrasting against her pale-blue skin tone.

She leapt towards me. Before I could even react, she had cupped my face in her hands. 'It's actually a human.' The girl smiled.

She blinked, and four more eyes appeared on her once-clear face. With all those eyes staring at me with such excitement, I couldn't help but feel a little afraid.

The six eyes protruding from her face disappeared as quickly as they appeared when Axon pulled her away from me. He gave me an apologetic smile. I felt my eyes narrow with distrust as I stared at them both.

'This is Elita,' Axon stated.

I nodded, 'Okay.'

Silence filled the room. Staring at this six-eyed girl reminded me of what was written in the journal. A word played on my tongue, strange and unknown still not quite believable.

'It is staring,' Elita whispered in awe.

'Aliens,' I said. 'You're aliens.'

Elita pursed her lips in a pouty manner, 'But there is human blood running through us.'

I took a step back. 'Why aren't I panicking? With everything that has happened, I'm still much more calm than afraid. The medication, the weird resistance group, my classmates and their hostility, the strange device that was strapped to my head…time travel…And now aliens? I'm way too calm.'

'It is just the drug,' Axon said matter-of-factly, waving his hand in the air as if shooing away a bug.

'But the drug's out of my system.'

'The drug still lingers in your system even though you feel as if you can control yourself again. So, at any time –'

'I could freak out like Danielle.' I said quietly.

It was obvious he didn't know who Danielle was from the sudden flash of confusion in his eyes but he still nodded and said, 'Exactly.'

So, now having a ticking time bomb of bothersome, unnecessary emotion to cloud my judgment added another complication to an already impossible situation. I wouldn't be able to think clearly, and (just like Danielle) I'd be silenced. I barely knew her, yet we were kind of alike in this way. *Well, she tried. I have to, too.* I took a deep breath and said, 'Either way, I've decided I'm going back to the past.'

'Do you know what you are going to do when you get there?' Elita asked.

'I'm going to get my brothers. We'll just lay low somewhere,' I paused. 'I know it's not going to be easy.'

'How are you going to get your brothers?' Axon asked. 'Everyone will be looking for you. They know what you look like.'

I shrugged. 'They shouldn't care so much if the future is going to remain unchanged.'

'Yes, but –'

'I know. I'll have to find a way.'

There was another small pause between us as I tried to think of ideas to get back into Albanrouke and get my brothers out. Elita glanced at Axon, her four eyes closing and disappearing within her face as her hair changed to a light blue. Everything about her seemed to change so easily. Without those extra eyes, she was fairly plain – almost unrecognisable. *If only I could change my appearance like that.* Then it hit me.

'This is the future, right?' I began. 'Is there any kind of technology that may be able to temporarily change my appearance?'

'There is, but it will not last long.' He explained.

'It lasts for about an hour,' Elita added.

'Then we should get going. I don't want to waste any more time.'

Again, Elita and Axon glanced at each other with worrisome expressions etched on their faces. He opened up the door, and I followed them down the corridor. We turned a sharp right and walked to a glass elevator.

'We are going down,' he said as we all stepped on.

'I have something to admit,' Elita blurted out. 'I am worried for my life. Just in case the future does change, will I exist?'

'Don't you remember?' My bitter voice filled the emptiness. 'Nothing will change.'

Nobody replied, and the hushed thrum of machinery sent us shooting downwards. The glass walls of the elevator slid down into small crevices in the floor as bright lights unveiled the room around us. The room was in the shape of a rhombus, its floors almost transparent with an underlying silver coating. There was a faint beeping sound coming from the stainless-steel chairs with white padded seats scattered around the room. On each chair was a small, silicone-ringed, face shield.

I traced my finger across the cool metal. 'So, this is it?'

Elita nodded. 'Yes, do you want to choose how you want to look?'

'I can do that?'

'Yes.' Elita smiled.

Elita swiped her hand against what I had assumed to be just air. A translucent screen displaying many categories describing the obvious selections of facial features appeared. It was a menu of different eyes, noses, lips, chins, and hair colours and styles. My fingertips struggled as they slid across the clear surface, finding it hard to browse and select. *There are too many choices!* I heard myself sighing too much. When I had the urge to punch the screen, I knew my frustration level was getting out of hand.

'Okay, okay,' Axon quickly said, stepping between the screen and me. 'Give me the general look you desire.'

I took a deep breath in an attempt to calm myself down. 'Long black hair, brown eyes.'

Axon quickly and effortlessly chose what I specified. I sat down in one of the seats and tried to prepare myself for what was to come without having a clue what that might be. Tapping the armrest with my finger nervously, I began to get increasingly annoyed at how emotional I was getting.

Elita brought down the device to fasten to my head, when, all of a sudden, an explosion of memories of the golden device that Ms McGuirk had planned to use on me assaulted my mind. The evil woman's wild, vacant eyes and waxy lips pulled into an amused grin sent chills up my spine. Mira, watching me with her own entertained smile, brought tears to my eyes.

I could feel the pain in my temples and I involuntarily shouted, 'Stop!' as I leanied back on the chair.

'What is wrong?' Axon asked with concern.

'Hold on a second.'

The golden rods protruding into my scalp. The blood trickling down my face. *Pain. So much pain. Make it stop.*

'Dylan?'

And then there was silence. And then I was running.

I blinked. 'I'm okay,' I cleared my throat.

'Are you sure?'

'Yes." *Breathe in. Breathe out.* 'Let's get this over with.'

Elita and Axon shared yet another worried glance.

With my jaw clenched and teeth grinding, I let the device descend upon my head, encasing me completely in what felt like a soft gel within. There was an intense tingling sensation all over my head for a couple of seconds before numbing down.

I looked up at Elita and Axon, expecting something else to happen, but she freed me from the device.

'Did it work?' I asked.

'Yes,' Axon said after a pause.

'Good, let's get going. You need to take me back exactly where you found me.'

'That will be easy, there is only one place.'

'Lead the way.'

Axon smiled and held out his hand to Elita.

She took it, her smile dwarfing all of her other features. 'This is my favourite part!'

I knew what he was going to do, and reluctantly I reached for the hand that he held out to me. Axon began to glow, golden tendrils travelling down his arms and attaching themselves to Elita and me. The glow brightened to an almost blinding light.

We were outside again.

We stood on dried-out sand, large cracks covering the ground like veins. In front of us was what appeared to be a large castle. Dark, slimy brickwork led up to a variety of blackened windows and shadowy outside stairways that even the two suns in the sky could not seem to brighten. Two outsized doors loomed over us.

Somehow, I knew this was the way back. I just hoped it could work. 'So, this is it.'

'I will miss you, human,' Elita smiled softly, her hair turning into a light red before darkening to black.

I wanted to reply in kind, but I didn't know her long enough for a sentimental farewell. It could be that she was overly fond of humans, but I would never know, never truly understand. Neither would I ever fully comprehend why they helped me when it could potentially destroy them if I managed to change the future.

Behind us, there appeared to be a small brick wall worn away to rubble with time but still standing high enough to create shade for those huddled under it. The hair on my arms pricked up as someone near the wall began to sharpen what I thought was an executioner's axe. His gaze was intent on the dull blade while sharp sounds of metal colliding against metal pierced my ears. Another person in the group took out a small boom box from underneath a pile of rags. He turned it on, and soft jazz music began to play an eerie and soulful soundtrack. The entire scene was bizarre and made more uncomfortable by the heat of the suns.

It was a strange group of people, all shaggy and content. I couldn't help but think that maybe they could be from another time, too. It could not have been kept in such pristine condition lying around in this environment. But I could be wrong, everything in this world was strange.

'Do you think it will work?' Axon asked.

I released the breath I was holding and nodded, 'Only one way to find out.'

I stepped forward and grabbed at the large doorknocker to pull it open. My hands, slipping with sweat, made it hard to grasp. I had to wipe my hands on my skirt a couple of times before there was a small popping sound. But instead of the large door opening, a smaller one did, its unseen frame and hinges hidden in the brickwork. I stared inside and saw the courtyard of the academy.

Gripping the journal tightly, I said, 'This is it.' I turned to face the two aliens. 'Thanks for the help.'

I didn't want to hear their reply. I didn't want to waste any more time. I walked through the door.

Chapter Six

The courtyard is silent. The sun's rays are shining down, creating a scene that belies the fear darkening the academy. As I cautiously take a step forward, autumn leaves crackle underneath my dirt-covered shoes. I look down and realise how dirty I am. People at the academy are always neat, clean, and dressed alike; I'm sure to stand out. I'm very lucky that everyone within the primary school will all be too drugged to notice my sloppy appearance.

With one last glance to the now bar-covered windows, I sprint to the left of the courtyard and enter the building where my brothers should both be. They won't remember me, but I'll still take them. As I walk the nearly empty halls, my heart begins to beat faster and faster with anxiety. Even though nobody will recognise me, I'm still in a very dangerous place.

I step between two lockers and flick through the journal to find the classroom my brothers are in. I need to check on them. I need to make sure they are okay before continuing my plan.

'E27,' I mutter to myself.

It's written inside. *Of course, it is.*

I'm still following the path that will lead to my eventual failure. I purse my lips. Even with this knowledge, I'm still determined to save them. *The future is not fixed. If I do just one unpredictable thing, everything else going forward can change.* I close the journal and saunter down the hallway, glancing at the room numbers until I reach one with the large letters I'm looking for.

I can see them through the door's window. Dark blonde hair, grey eyes – exactly like me, and surrounded by other eleven-year-olds all sharing the same blank expression on their young and innocent faces. But one thing is different. The teacher isn't talking either. Just like the students, she stares blankly. Her eyes are glazed over like everyone else's. *Has Ms McGuirk begun to drug the teachers? Shouldn't they have already been turned by now?*

A small sigh of relief escapes my lips as I wipe my hands across my skirt. I'm much safer than before, but still not safe enough. Stepping back from the door, I flick through the journal again. Words move across the pages, letters and numbers forming new sentences that now describe the actions I had just taken to return to Albanrouke. The future is already changing.

I quickly read down a couple of lines until I find David and Jeremy's dorm numbers. They are just down the hall from each other. So, with a quick glance at my watch to confirm ne time, I swiftly move down the hall and open the door to the next building where I will wait in the closest dorm room: Jeremy's.

Ten minutes until classes end for the day. Thirty minutes until the disguise wears off. And three hours until we can escape.

The dorm building is empty except for a few cleaners walking about the place. Their glassy eyes tell me that they have been turned, not drugged; the drugs are no longer necessary after a person has been turned. So, if they see me, they would tell Ms McGuirk immediately. My plan would be over.

I duck into a nearby doorway as one of them walks past, the sound of his mechanised trudging filling in the emptiness. I wait there until I can't hear them anymore. Moving quickly, I turn left and open the door of the first room on the left.

Jeremy's bedroom is exactly like mine, right down to the small bin next to his desk. I close the door and sit down on the bed.

Five minutes left.

Flicking through the journal, I can see that David's bedroom is four doors down. This will make it easier for me, but who knows what could happen in the future. My heart continues to beat excessively within the silence, and I have to wipe my sweaty palms on my skirt repeatedly. A strange sensation in my eyes gets stronger until small tears parade down my cheeks. I feel like I am running out of time and there is nothing I can do.

My failure – the one everyone from the future kept telling me about – feels so far away, and yet so close. *But maybe I'll be okay. Maybe my brothers will be okay. Right?*

Right?

I sniffle, wiping my tears and nose with my sleeve. I just need to have hope. *I've come this far already. Why back out now?*

Well, why not? You're going to fail. Just give in. Was life so bad before? Sure, you were drugged, but you were alive. Are you going to still be alive after this? Who knows? Just give in. Who cares if aliens take over the world?

WHO.

CARES.

Not your parents, that's for sure! They're the ones who put you here in the first place.

Where are you going to go once you leave? Not crying to Mummy and Daddy, that's for su –

The door opens.

I jump to my feet and dart forward. Skin and material collide as I push him away from the door. With his blank eyes staring at me, I quickly grab onto his wrist and pull him towards David's room.

My breath catches in my throat when I see that David has already gone inside, the door slowly closing behind him. With a couple of more rushed steps, I quickly jam my foot between the door and doorframe to keep it from closing. I drag Jeremy inside just as the door closes behind us.

And there we all are, reunited. The three Inarkaevich children are together once again.

I sit Jeremy and David on the bed, their blank faces continuing to unnerve me. I feel that, through their gazes, the others can see me. *But that can't be possible, can it?*

The sound of a click behind me and the alarm ringing let me know that we're locked in until dinner. By the time we're released, my disguise will be gone.

All I can to do now is wait.

'I'm going to get us out of here,' I tell them.

Silence is their response. Now I know how Mira felt that day in the cafeteria: the judgement, the sadness, the paranoia.

'I wish you guys could reply.'

**

Sitting in silence and waiting for the inevitable escape is something like struggling to stay afloat in the ocean at night with a small life preserver. Waves of hope and happiness wash over me as I cling to the safety of possible escape. But then an undertow of fear and danger is ever-present, threatening to pull me down once and for all.

I don't know how to react to it. It's strange feeling this way. Or feeling anything.

My left eye keeps twitching. My hands and legs are trembling, and my heart is reckless in how many times it beats per second. I feel as if any moment I could cry. But the most annoying thing of all is the heat. I can't stop sweating. My hands are wet with a slick layer of perspiration. I have to keep wiping my hands. *What if, somehow, I lose my brothers because I can't keep a tight grip on them?* I catch my reflection in the mirror and watch as my hair changes from black back to blonde. My eyes return to their original grey. The insufferable heat subsides, but my heart hasn't stopped racing. *I can be recognised now.*

I glance over at my brothers' young faces, unquestioning and unaware. *How long will it take for the drug to get out of their systems? One day? Two days?* I can't remember what I was told.

In a few moments, the alarm will sound and the door will unlock. My plan is to run to the main entrance of the school, straight past the front desk and outside into the world.

Away. We just have to get away.

The sound of the alarm fills my ears and I slowly stand up. I can feel my legs buckling beneath me, but I do my best to ignore it.

'It's time to go,' I tell them.

I grab their hands and pull them up and out into the hall. Tugging them down the crowded passageway, we try to blend in amidst the drugged primary school students heading towards the cafeteria for dinner. I keep thinking I might be recognised, but I continually remind myself that only high school students get turned. Here, they're drugged while they're still being prepared.

But that fact does little to alleviate my fear.

The sound of my quickening breaths and rapid footsteps, followed by those of my clueless brothers, echo through the silence of the hallway. Even being surrounded by students, it is easy to maneuver ourselves past the front desk and in front of the main doors. They are all drugged senseless, after all.

It seems too easy.

I glance over at the receptionist who watches us with an amused grin on his lips. His dark brown hair is braided, and his brown eyes stare steadily ahead. Sporting a goatee, he looks more intimidating than he needs to be.

He leans back in his chair and licks his lips. 'No, no, keep doing what you are doing,' he says in an amused voice. 'The door is wide open.'

'You won't stop us,' I state, but it feels like more of a question.

His smile only grows larger. 'Go ahead. See what happens.'

My breath catches in my throat as I look back at the door. Keeping a firm grip on my brothers' hands, I press my lips together and step forward. The door slides open automatically when sensing my presence. I still can feel the eyes of the receptionist staring at the back of my head, but there is no reason to delay this any further.

I step outside. We step outside.

**

The air is different out here, the oppressive atmosphere is trapped behind the now-closed front doors to Albanrouke. I take a deep breath and enjoy the wind blowing through my hair.

It's strange to think so much has changed, and I wish that Jeremy and David knew how things once were. But they don't.

Which is strange. From what I remember, it only took about fifteen minutes for me to regain my thoughts and my speech when I had forgotten to take the tablet that day. *Why haven't they spoken yet?* Maybe they don't see this situation as important. Maybe they don't remember me, so they feel shy and nervous. I release my grip on their hands and turn to them. The road we're walking beside is empty except for a few cars that drive past us every so often, and I feel an ever-increasing distance between my brothers and me.

'Aren't you wondering why you're both not inside Albanrouke anymore?' I ask. 'Aren't you wondering why I took you out?'

Their eyes judge me, but still they haven't said a word.

I sigh and take my backpack off, reaching inside until I feel the familiar leather cover on my fingertips. I take it out and flip through the last few pages of my section in the 'Problems' area. The words have changed. They describe my encounter with the receptionist and soon fade with the description of us leaving the school. Now, we're on our own.

'I think you guys can follow me all on your own now, huh?' I ask.

I can already tell what they're trying to do. I would have been the same. We all would have been the same.

'So, you've assessed the situation and realised you have absolutely no knowledge of it. I suppose I can't blame you for closing down on me. I'd do the same if I were in your situation. But let's face it, you have nowhere else to go, and you don't know how to go back. You're stuck, so you might as well just come with me. I'll tell you everything once we get settled.' I place the journal back in my backpack. 'Come on then.'

I step backwards a few steps and wait for them to follow. Their eyes still question me, but I stare relentlessly until they take a few steps towards me. I feel my lips turn upwards into a smile. We continue walking down the road, appearing to be three agreeable travellers. I can't help but tense every time a car drives past. *What if the people within are turned? What if they are watching me and reporting back?*

The streets become busy as day turns into night. 'People' leave and enter homes and various buildings that line each side of the road. Frequently, I check back to see if Jeremy and David are still with me. I'm relieved to see the drug is beginning to leave their systems. We have to slow our pace because they're looking around so much, their eyes glistening with curiosity as they take in the world around them. I envy them. *I should be enjoying this freedom, too.*

I look to the right and see a large white sign with dark green letters reading, 'Great Valley Holiday Park.' Underneath is large cream-coloured building. Families with children under five-years-old are walking in and out, pulling suitcases behind them. Obviously, this is a place to stay overnight.

'What do you think?' I ask, nodding toward the building.

Yet again, silence is their reply.

Then, a soft sound escapes someone's lips. My eyes widen, and I turn around to face them. There's no sign that either of them spoke at all.

'I want to go back,' Jeremy says.

A few tears trickle down my face. Almost imperceptibly, I shake my head. 'No.'

'I want to go back,' he repeats.

'You're staying with me. You're both staying with me.'

I grab their hands and pull them through the front doors. Inside, a woman sits at a front desk and welcomes those walking past. We share a brief smile before her voice calls out to me. 'Excuse me.'

Is she one of them? I immediately put on a smile and turn around. 'Yes?'

The woman quickly grabs my hand and places a stamp on it. 'I hope you have a great afternoon here.'

Yes, right...the afternoon. 'Thanks. Yes. We will.' I nod.

She stamps both Jeremy's and David's hands while looking down at them with a smile when she notices David's distant face. 'Is he okay?'

I glance at my brothers and back at her. 'Yeah, I just have to get him back to Mum and Dad before he throws another fit.'

'What does he have?'

I feel my forehead dampen with sweat as I search my mind for an answer. 'Pervasive development disorder,' I answer. 'He has a pervasive development disorder.'

'I see,' she said. 'Make sure to find your parents soon, okay?'

'Okay.'

Her facial expression seems almost empathetic to David's fake mental disorder, but I can feel her judging me. *Does she know I'm lying?*

I can still feel her eyes on me as we walk into the park.

Chapter Seven

The scene before us is a canvas painted in happiness. Families eat together at various barbecues, children play on the playgrounds and are followed around by over-protective mothers. Some couples have rowed out onto the lake and are either relaxing or fishing. Others have travelled farther down to where various other colourful attractions stand, children gaping at the water slides and playing in the dirt. On the left side of the park is a large, winding path leading to a bunch of cabins, tents and even trailers for people who have decided to stay the night. I almost want to believe this is my reality, but it isn't.

I don't fit in here. Neither do my brothers.

We're too old. All the children are under five, which means that they haven't been taken to a 'school' yet. That also means that my brothers and I stand out like daisies among a field of weeds. Two eleven-year-olds and a seventeen-year-old. We should be in an academy, not roaming around the countryside. *I should have thought of that.*

They have to know. They have to know we aren't supposed to be here.

'Do you notice anything?' I ask my brothers.

'I want to go back,' Jeremy states again.

I ignore his comment and glance at David. His facial expression is a riddle of competing emotions. My best guess is a mix of awe and suspicion. He doesn't understand what's wrong.

'We are not supposed to be here,' Jeremy continues.

'I know, but that's not going to change anything.' I pause. 'Do you think they're watching us?'

'Depends.'

They could be watching us for entertainment purposes. Even now, I can picture the smirk on Mira's lips as she told me to run. For a second, I thought she wanted to help me, but I knew deep down she never wanted me to make it. She just wanted to see me try.

Is that what's happening now, too?

Anybody in this park could be turned, and they all could be watching. Every. Single. One.

'Let's find a place to stay and rest,' I say, walking down the path towards the cabins.

My brothers follow me obediently. Upon closer inspection, the cabins appear worn and decrepit. Smudges cover the windows, making it hard to get a clear view inside. The timbered exterior panels are slightly gnawed away; a couple have even fallen loose and lay on the soft rass below. It's as if nobody has stayed here for years, and are only looked after every couple of weeks. Enough to make them habitable, but not enough to feel comfortable or even entirely safe. Couples and families with young kids are leaving or entering some of them. *Why are there still so many people here? Do they notice us? Do they care?*

'I guess we could choose any of the empty ones.' I shrug.

Silence, yet again.

My eyes centre on the cabin on the far left at the end of the path. It's a bit more ragged compared to the others but still acceptable. I look back at my brothers and, with a slight nod, they know which cabin I've chosen. I hurry towards it.

I inspect the hinges on the locked door to determine if the door opens out towards us or inwardly. Luckily, it is the latter. I aim my foot beside the lock and kick. It bursts open.

'Come on,' I say as I go inside.

We are welcomed by a large double bed within what appears to be the neatly made-up living room. To the right, is a small couch and television. On top of the TV is a DVD player and a couple of free in-house movies, all are equally unused and covered in a layer of dust. In the second bedroom, there is one bunk bed and a single bed. The bedding and towels are folded neatly on top of each bed as if waiting for somebody's arrival.

The tiny kitchen is equipped with a microwave, cook top and a mini-fridge. Checking each one, they all appear to be working. The cupboards and draws contain crockery, cutlery and saucepans. On one of the benches, there is a kettle and a toaster ready to be used.

Even the bathroom has more than the basics for living the life of a traveler. There is a hairdryer. Leaning against one of the walls is an ironing board and iron. Everything is prepared for guests, right down to what may have been the welcome tea, coffee and sugar.

The atmosphere is strange, though. I sense an emptiness in what seemed to be a space begging to be lived in once again. A temporary stop-over that wanted to be a permanent home. A place filled with fleeting, sad memories that longed for lasting, cheerier ones.

'This seems suitable,' I say. 'What do you think?'

'What will we eat?' David asks, unimpressed.

'Just join in on the barbecues outside.'

I swipe my hand over the couch in some silly attempt to clean the dust before I sit down. As I stare at my brothers, I grow more troubled by their still-confused faces when they take in the scene around them. *They probably don't even know who I am.*

'I'm Dylan,' I begin. 'I'm your sister.'

Chapter Eight

Jeremy and David run about the small cabin with smiles on their faces and sparkling eyes. It's nice to see them carefree, the way children should be. I stretch out my legs and then bring my knees to my chest. I've been sitting for a while, and my legs are a bit sore. But I'm not going to move out of this cabin. I peek through the blinds and watch all the people outside. They probably have all been turned and are keeping an eye on us. *They must be so amused.*

I watch.

I wait.

But for how long?

How long?

How long?

How long?

How long?

How long?

HOW LONG?

HOW LONG?

HOW MUCH TIME TO DO WE WA –

'Dylan?' Jeremy calls out.

My breath catches in my throat 'Yeah?'

'We are hungry.'

I peer through the blinds once again. Everyone outside is sitting on small tables near the barbecues watching various musicians perform. I look back at my brothers' young faces. They at least deserve to have the kind of normal childhood I remember reading about in books in the school library – the kind of childhood with family barbecues. They should experience it at least once.

'Go out and get some food with everyone else,' I say. 'But don't speak to anyone, and as soon as you get some food, you come straight back.'

'Thanks,' the boys reply in unison as they run out onto the green grass.

They seem so happy. So clueless.

I watch them as they follow the line of people to the pans of freshly cooked food. I watch them as they grab three plates and fill them up. I watch them open their mouths when replying to those talking them. I watch their nervous gazes meet mine when they know I caught them talking, and I watch them briskly walk back to me with full plates.

'We are back,' David greets me as they enter the room.

'I know.' A small smile lifts the corners of my lips.

They place the plates on the table and list the foods they have been able to bring inside to eat.

'Come eat with us.' David invites me over to the table.

I shake my head. 'Just bring my plate here.'

'Please,' Jeremy adds.

'Fine.' My throat feels tight as I try to keep my voice from quivering.

I trudge toward them and stop beside the table. Trying to peer past their heads, my attempt to look through the window to see what the others are doing fails. The blinds conceal my view.

Jeremy and David exchange glances as I begin to eat.

'I saw you guys speak to the others outside,' I comment. 'What did you speak about?'

'They asked why I had a third plate, so I told them you were waiting inside,' Jeremy answers.

'Why? Is it really that important?'

'Bu –'

'I told you not to speak to them. Why don't you understand? I've explained everything,' I pause. 'We have to leave.'

The boys share worried looks once again, 'When was the last time you slept?' David asks.

'I don't need sleep.'

Yes, you do.

No, I don't. I need to protect my brothers.

You cannot protect anyone while sleep-deprived.

I need to stay awake. I need to keep watch. That's more important than sleep.

No, it is not. You will die.

I don't want to have that dream again. I need to protect them.

'It's important that you two get some sleep, not me.'

'What if we all get some sleep? Together?' David speaks again.

'No. That's not a good idea.'

I look down at my plate; it's nearly empty and the afternoon light is fading. Shadows cover our faces and the surfaces of objects around us. *This place is dangerous.* It feels almost surreal.

Everywhere feels dangerous. Everywhere is dangerous.

'We will sleep with the light on.' Jeremy adds.

A light will draw attention.

'Okay,' I said.

Jeremy stands up and grabs my hand, pulling me over to the bed and sitting me down. David follows. 'The three of us together, okay, Sis?'

I don't want to sleep, but I want them to be happy.

Maybe just a few minutes will be okay.

I nod and lie down on the bed. A couple of seconds later, Jeremy and David join me. I pull them into a hug and allow my eyelids to finally close.

**

Voices whisper within the night and slowly awaken me. Jeremy and David are gone from the bed. My heart rate speeds up, and I whirl around to see them sitting at the table. Their heads are hung low, their voices soft and hushed.

'What's going on?' I ask, my voice thick from the daze of sleep.

Their heads snap up and they stare at me wide-eyed, but only for a moment. Their spontaneous and simultaneous knee-jerk reaction disappears into eerily calm little smiles. Identical, calm little smiles.

'I got up to have some water and woke up David. We have just been talking.'

'Really?'

'Yes,' David agrees, 'we did not want to wake you.'

I scan the table. 'Where's the glass?'

Jeremy looks down at his hands and back at me. 'Um...in the sink.'

I swallow the growing lump in my throat. 'Come back to bed. It's late.'

I lie down and wait until I can feel their bodies next to mine before I close my eyes.

**

A loud banging sound fills my ears, awakening me from my slumber. I groggily get up and look around. A soft light comes through the blinds. It's early morning.

'Guys, what's going on?' I ask.

I look down beside me expecting to see my brothers, but only Jeremy is there. His eyes are wide open as he lies completely still. Only the up-and-down movement of his chest tells me he's alive.

The banging sound is getting louder.

'Jeremy,' I ask, 'where's David?'

Jeremy glances at me, and quickly sits up, 'Dylan I'm –'

The front door bursts open and a group of seven or eight people come inside. Domineering and formidable, they immediately block all exits and turn to face me. I scramble backwards, pushing Jeremy behind me.

'Nice to see you again, Miss Inarkaevich.' A man begins to speak to me in a tone one might use to approach a crazy person with a dangerous weapon – measured, insincere, patronising. 'We thought it was about time to pick you up. It was fun watching you for a while but now it has become quite boring.'

'Stay awa –'

'I am sorry, Dylan,' Jeremy meekly interrupts.

'What?' I turn to face him.

His eyes wide and full of tears, he repeats himself.

'What do you mean? Where's David?'

Jeremy won't look at me, and I watch as he frees himself from my grip and stands with the group of strangers in our cabin.

'You can't be serious!' I stand up and clench my fists. 'You can't be serious!'

Jeremy continues to avoid my gaze. From behind him, a boy with the same guilty face steps out. David.

'You did the right thing boys,' the man says.

I bite my lip and look straight at my brothers.

I'm not going to stop staring at them. I'm going to force them to look at me.

'How dare you? After everything I've done, and you do this? You joined them! I can't...I can't believe this.' I wipe the tears from my face and march right up to them. 'After this is over, you're going to regret everything.'

I raise my fist and punch the man in the stomach.

The others pounce on me before I have time to throw another punch or kick.

What happens next is pandemonium for me. My limbs are pulled. Someone yanks my hands behind my back. I'm forced down to my knees. Then my head is pushed down.

I struggle to fight back. I get one leg up.

I can't let them get me!

I feel a grinding pressure pushing into my back.

My body hits the ground.

With my cheek pressed to the floor, I can only see out of one bruised eye. The golden device is pulled out.

'I hope you're both happy,' I seethe.

It's pressed hard onto my head.

'Now!' The man boomed out the order.

I can't save them. I can't even save myself.

I scream.

'Hi, Mum.'

The End.